The Music Inside My Heart

The Musical
Adventures Of
GREY GOOSE

Written by
LISA BUSBICE BOSS

Illustrated by
CHAD THOMPSON

◆ FriesenPress

Suite 300 - 990 Fort St
Victoria, BC, V8V 3K2
Canada

www.friesenpress.com

ISBN
978-1-5255-4279-4 (Hardcover)
978-1-5255-4280-0 (Paperback)
978-1-5255-4281-7 (eBook)

1. JUVENILE FICTION, PERFORMING ARTS, MUSIC

Distributed to the trade by The Ingram Book Company

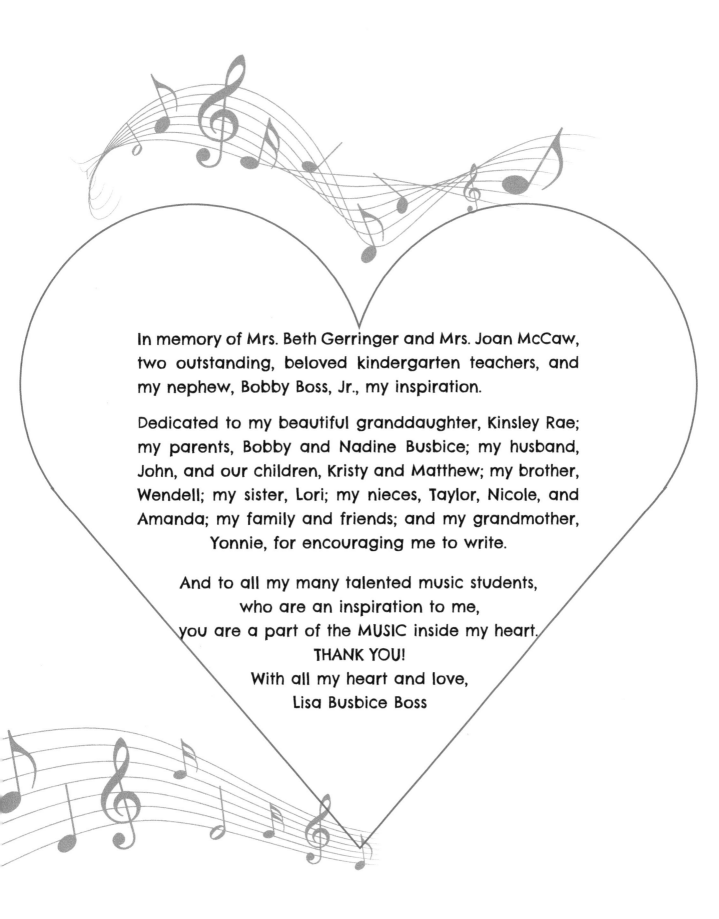

In memory of Mrs. Beth Gerringer and Mrs. Joan McCaw, two outstanding, beloved kindergarten teachers, and my nephew, Bobby Boss, Jr., my inspiration.

Dedicated to my beautiful granddaughter, Kinsley Rae; my parents, Bobby and Nadine Busbice; my husband, John, and our children, Kristy and Matthew; my brother, Wendell; my sister, Lori; my nieces, Taylor, Nicole, and Amanda; my family and friends; and my grandmother, Yonnie, for encouraging me to write.

And to all my many talented music students, who are an inspiration to me, you are a part of the MUSIC inside my heart. THANK YOU! With all my heart and love, Lisa Busbice Boss

It was the first day of school, on a cool, sunny day, in early September. The leaves were starting to turn different colors. Kinsley had been waiting for this day for almost forever. Two weeks before school started, Kinsley had laid out her favorite pink flowered dress with her matching pink sparkle shoes and her pink bow for her hair. She was going to look like a princess on her first day of school. She couldn't wait to ride the school bus and to be a third grader at Harmony Park Elementary School.

Kinsley didn't sleep very well the night before, as she was so excited and ready to start her school day. Grammy and Pop Pop made Kinsley her favorite breakfast of pancakes smothered in syrup, sweet pineapple chunks, and a cup of mango juice. She loved every bite!

After breakfast, Kinsley hugged and kissed her mommy good-bye as she entered the school bus. As the bus pulled away, she waved to her mommy.

Very soon Kinsley's bus arrived at Harmony Park Elementary School. The children got off and were greeted by a tall man. "I'm Mr. Robert McCaw, the superintendent of schools," he said. "These are your two principals, Mrs. Kalin and Dr. Straw, and this is the assistant-principal, Dr. Via."

There were other staff members too. They greeted Kinsley and the other children by giving them big waves as they got off the buses. As Kinsley made her way through the front doors of the school, she felt warm and happy inside.

Kinsley met her third-grade teacher, Mrs. Gerringer. Mrs. Gerringer was a very popular teacher. She was a kind, gentle, friendly lady and welcomed everyone to her classroom. Most of the third graders knew her already, as they'd had her as a teacher in kindergarten. The children were excited that the kindergarten teacher they LOVED so much was teaching third grade. They felt lucky to have her again as their teacher. The children liked the way Mrs. Gerringer always had a smile on her face, and she was so excited about everything. She was funny and liked to tell jokes. She loved making the children laugh, always making everyone feel so special.

After seeing Mrs. Gerringer, Kinsley saw her best friends Kristy, Margaret, Nadine, Audrey, and Trina hanging their jackets up under their cubbies. Kinsley and her friends sang in the youth choir at church. All the girls had dreams of becoming singers one day.

Kinsley ran up to her friends and said, "We're in the same class! I'm so EXCITED! Mrs. Gerringer was my favorite teacher when I was in kindergarten and she is so COOL!"

"YES! Mrs. Gerringer is so nice and an AWESOME teacher!" Kristy said. The girls all hugged each other, beaming with joy!

Bob, Wendell, and Dave, who had dreams of playing football for the University of Maryland someday, came in next. They were talking about their football team, the Terps. They had won their first game on Saturday. They shared the good news with Mrs. Gerringer, who congratulated the three boys. "Go Terps!" she said.

Mrs. Gerringer welcomed the next group of girls. Lori, Taylor, Nicole, and Amanda were talking about their fun day spent at the end-of-the-summer pool party on Labor Day. The girls loved to swim. They had dreams of becoming Olympic swimmers and winning a bunch of gold medals. All four girls were sad that the pool had closed for the season.

Next into the room came Bobby Junior, John, and Matt. Bobby Junior had his basketball with him. He had dreams of becoming a pro basketball player. John and Matt loved to go fishing. They dreamed of becoming pro fishermen and becoming master chefs in their own restaurant.

"Hello boys," said Mrs. Gerringer.

"Hello, Mrs. Gerringer!" said the boys.

Bobby Junior placed his basketball above his cubby. "Let's play at recess," he said to his friends.

"Let's do it!" said John and Matt. They placed their lunches on the lunch cart.

"I hope lunch comes around sooner rather than later," Matt said with a smile.

Nancy and June had dreams of sewing in their own fashion shop. They ran up to Mrs. Gerringer and said at the same time, "Mrs. Gerringer, do you like our new dresses?"

"Yes, I do! Your dresses are beautiful, just like you!" said Mrs. Gerringer.

"Thank you, Mrs. Gerringer!" both girls replied.

"We bought them at our new favorite store in town called Sew For Fun!" Nancy said, as both girls twirled around in circles.

"I'll have to go shopping there one day," said Mrs. Gerringer.

Louise, Joan, and Diane, who knew each other from the public library club, waved at Mrs. Gerringer. They walked right past the two twirling girls to place their favorite books in their cubbies. They were hoping to read their books later. The girls had dreams of becoming reading teachers.

Joe, Anne, Jenny, and Susie burst into the room playing their kazoos. They loved music! They took private piano lessons from the same piano teacher. Mrs. Gerringer bobbed her head to the beat of the piece they were playing as they rushed on by. These children hoped to be performing in concerts on stage one day. They dreamed of becoming stars!

Mrs. Gerringer waved to the next group of boys, who were deep in conversation with each other. Wayne, Jim, Chris, Charlie, Martin, and Paul loved to play with Legos. They dreamed of making cars, trucks, planes, and tall buildings. They were talking about what they were going to build next. They placed their lunches on the lunch cart and continued their conversation as they took a seat on the carpet.

Gail, Kim, Sandy, Janice, Terri, and Laurie met up with Colleen, Debbie, Joyce, Beverly, Kris, and Vicky down the hallway from Mrs. Gerringer's classroom. They had a surprise gift to give to Mrs. Gerringer. The girls belonged to the same gym team at the community rec center. They dreamed about being future teachers and leaders in America. They couldn't wait to join the local 4-H Club.

As the girls walked up to Mrs. Gerringer, they shouted, "SURPRISE!" They presented Mrs. Gerringer with a beautiful bouquet of flowers.

"Thank you, girls. WOW! What gorgeous flowers!" said Mrs. Gerringer.

Jane, who loved to draw pictures, had her artwork displayed in a showcase in the front of the school. She had drawn a portrait of a Native American family. Everyone who entered the school admired her beautiful picture. Jane dreamed of becoming an artist. She gave Mrs. Gerringer a beautiful picture she had created of herself holding hands with Mrs. Gerringer, in front of the school. They were both smiling and wore beautiful, multi-colored floral dresses with matching turquoise shoes. In the background of Jane's picture was a blue sky, a colorful rainbow, a bright yellow sun, a few birds, and lots of flowers. At the top of her picture were the words, WE LOVE YOU, MRS. GERRINGER!

Someone had scribbled that same message on the chalkboard.

Mrs. Gerringer was very surprised to receive such lovely gifts. She thanked the girls again for their kindness. All the students were eager to start the first day of school. Mrs. Gerringer welcomed all her students again and invited the children to sit with her on the carpet in the front of the classroom.

"Please settle down, children," said Mrs. Gerringer. "I want to introduce you to someone very special. This is Mrs. McCaw. She's going to help me teach all of you."

"Well hello there, everybody," said Mrs. McCaw with a big, friendly smile.

The children liked her right away.

Mrs. Gerringer and Mrs. McCaw let the children know about their schedules for the day. Kinsley would go to reading, math, lunch, recess, science, and then it was time for related arts. Related arts classes were art, media, music, P.E., and technology. Today the class would be going to music. Kinsley LOVED music! She LOVED singing and playing instruments. At home, Kinsley loved playing her xylophone while Grammy played her guitar and Pop Pop played his harmonica. But her favorite part was when they sang as many songs as they could sing.

It was finally time for music. Kinsley could hardly wait! Mrs. Boss, the music teacher, was standing outside the music room ready to greet the children. As soon as the children saw Mrs. Boss, they excitedly rushed over to her and gave her a huge group hug. Mrs. Boss had been their music teacher since kindergarten. As the children entered the music room, they noticed that the room was decorated with many beautifully colored music posters, musical bulletin boards, and brightly colored musical notes dangling, hanging, or stuck on the walls. The music room was filled with musical instruments of every kind. There was a piano and a guitar, drums of all sizes, xylophones, metallophones, glockenspiels, recorders, and rhythm-band instruments of rhythm sticks, tambourines, cymbals, claves, jingles, triangles, woodblocks, sand blocks, and maracas. Mrs. Boss had a big smile on her face. She was excited about the children being in music.

Mrs. Boss showed the children a small, beautiful plush toy. It looked more like a duck, but she called him Grey Goose. Grey Goose had a speckled gray and white color on his body and on his wings, with a white chest, black eyes, and bright orange webbed feet and beak. He lived in a basket decorated in colorful musical-note fabric on Mrs. Boss' desk. He LOVED to sing and dance with the children every day in music. Mrs. Boss let the children hold Grey Goose as she told the class about some of the musical activities they would be participating in throughout the school year. The children were excited about singing, moving, dancing, listening, and playing instruments, as well as creating and learning to read music. Mrs. Boss told the class that it was their job to try their best in all the activities.

Mrs. Boss opened up the music lesson with a greeting song called "Welcome, My Friend." The children recognized the song and immediately started singing. Mrs. Boss had the class clap the beat to the song. Some of the children remembered the hand-clapping pattern that Mrs. Boss had taught them last year. The children were already finding partners. They clapped their own hands and then clapped their partner's hands to the beat. Mrs. Boss encouraged all the children to do the hand-clapping pattern with a partner to the beat of the song. In the middle of the song, Mrs. Boss said, "Two, four, six, eight, ten, find a new friend and we'll sing it again!" The children switched partners, and they repeated singing the song, performing the hand-clapping pattern with their new partners.

After the song, Mrs. Boss asked, "What is a beat?"

Wendell whispered, "A vegetable?"

The class giggled softly.

"A beat is a steady, repeated pulse in music!" Anne blurted out.

"That's correct Anne. Good for you!" said Mrs. Boss. Anne was a brilliant piano, cello, and French horn player. At a very young age, she already performed on those instruments.

Mrs. Boss said, "A beat of a song is like your heart beat. Just like Anne said, a beat is the steady, repeating pulse of the music. The steady beat can be very fast, fast, moderate, slow, or a very slow tempo. Tempo is determined by the speed of the beat. If the beat of the music is fast, the tempo will be fast. If the beat of the music is moderate, the tempo will be of a medium speed. If the beat of the music is slow, the tempo will be slow. The same goes for very fast and very slow beats. Sometimes the beat can get gradually faster or slower. You have to feel the pulse of the music and then clap your hands or tap your foot to the beat."

Mrs. Boss played some examples of different beats on the piano and other instruments. The children identified the beat by tapping their two fingers into the palm of their other hand. Mrs. Boss then played her guitar to the beat, getting faster and slower. The song she played was called the "March Game" song. The children laughed and marched, jumped, or stomped to match the different tempos of the beat. It was a FUN game to play! Kinsley loved the "March Game" song, especially when Mrs. Boss strummed a chord on the guitar while saying the word "march" to a slow, steady beat. Then the beat slowly changed and got faster and faster, until the beat got so fast, the children couldn't get the word "march" out fast enough to keep up. The children loved running to the beat when it got so fast that they all dropped to the floor, giggling and laughing. Grey Goose had fun too!

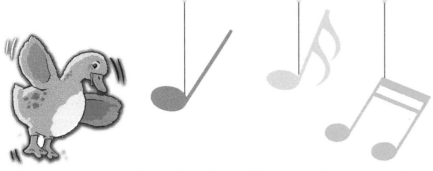

It was time for the children to sing the "Harmony Park School Song." The children knew this song as they had learned it in kindergarten. They sang the refrain of the song. The refrain of a song is a repeated part that is sung over and over again.

Mrs. Boss said, "If you know this song, just sing along!"

The children sang the words:

"Harmony Park is AWESOME, FUN, a school where you will find,

Science, Tech, Engineering, Math, and Arts expand your mind.

When you enter Harmony Park, you'll see a friendly smile,

Harmony Park's the BEST SCHOOL for one hundred million miles!"

After they sang the song many times, Mrs. Boss put some movements to the song and the children and Grey Goose sang the song with pride!

Kim said, "My sisters Rita and DonnaMarie sing this song all the time. Sometimes DonnaMarie plays her accordion as they sing. Musically, they sound AWESOME! Well . . . my sisters told me that a group of fifth graders wrote the song a few years ago. Is that true?"

Mrs. Boss replied, "Yes, the song was written long before I arrived at Harmony Park Elementary School. History has it that it was written by a group of fifth graders, and the students loved the song so much that it became the official school song."

Mrs. Boss asked, "What makes Harmony Park the BEST SCHOOL for one hundred million miles?"

The children gave answers like, "Good food." "Nice building." "Great teachers."

"I have an idea," said Mrs. Boss. "In the next few weeks, I'll hide Grey Goose around the school. If you can find Grey Goose, look around you for clues for the answer to my question. Grey Goose will help you find the answer. Then return Grey Goose to me. Class, I will miss Grey Goose as he wanders on his journey throughout the school. Good luck in your search to find him!"

The next day the children ran into the classroom. They looked in their cubbies for Grey Goose. "Not here!" yelled Kinsley.

They looked for Grey Goose everywhere. They looked underneath their desks and in the play area. Kinsley even looked on top of Mrs. Gerringer's desk, but no one could find him. They went to reading and did not see him in the reading classroom.

Where could Grey Goose be?

The children lined up and went down to the cafeteria for lunch. They continued to search for Grey Goose. The children looked underneath the tables, behind the recycling bins, and around the food being served in the lunch line. There on top of the ice-cream machine was GREY GOOSE! The children squealed with delight at finding Grey Goose. They could not wait to return him to Mrs. Boss in her music classroom. When Mrs. Gerringer said it was time to go to music, the children cheered very loudly.

Upon entering the music room, Kinsley was chosen to carry Grey Goose to Mrs. Boss. Kinsley was so excited! She knew Mrs. Boss would be so happy that the class had found her Grey Goose. The children looked at Mrs. Boss with HUGE SMILES on their faces. Mrs. Boss knew something was going on. The children sat down on the floor of the music room, and Mrs. Boss played the chords on the piano to start music. She asked the class if they had found Grey Goose. With that, Kinsley stood up and gave Grey Goose to Mrs. Boss. The children all clapped their hands with JOY, as Mrs. Boss cheered with them.

rs. Boss asked the class, "So, what clue did Grey Goose give you to answer my question? What makes Harmony Park the BEST SCHOOL for one hundred million miles?"

The children replied, "Our school has the BEST LUNCHES!"

Underneath the question she had written on the board, Mrs. Boss wrote Best Lunches.

Mrs. Boss said, "Yes, the lunches at Harmony Park are excellent, but keep searching for Grey Goose. You have not quite found the answer to my question yet. So, let's sing! If you know this song . . ."

"Just sing along!" the children shouted.

The children sang the "Harmony Park School Song" to open up the music lesson. Grey Goose sat on top of the piano, listening to the children's beautiful voices as they sang the song.

In the next activity, the children found the BEAT of an orchestral piece by moving to a John Philip Sousa march, "Stars and Stripes Forever." Mrs. Boss grabbed Grey Goose and led the children down the hallway and around the inside of the school, while the children marched to the steady beat. When they returned to the music classroom, the piece was still playing, and the children were still marching to the steady beat. Mrs. Boss chose different students to lead the class in creating their own movements to the beat.

After the movement activity, Mrs. Boss explained how the famous piece "Stars and Stripes Forever" had been composed by John Philip Sousa in 1896. That was a long time ago, before the children were even born. In 1987, through an act of the U.S. Congress, the piece became the official National March of the U.S.A.

It was instrument time! Mrs. Boss went over and picked up her huge musical bag. It was filled to the brim with musical instruments. Inside her musical bag were rhythm sticks, jingles, maracas, woodblocks, sand blocks, cymbals, claves, triangles, tambourines, xylophones, and drums of all shapes and sizes. As Mrs. Boss handed each student an instrument, she named each instrument. Then she played it to show the class how to produce the sound. Kinsley was handed a tambourine. She started shaking it right away.

"Class, please put your instruments in your lap for a nap," said Mrs. Boss. By this, she meant for them to keep the instruments silent. Kinsley put her instrument in her lap.

Mrs. Boss put an African rhythm chart on the board. There were eight numbered lines on the chart, and each line had the numbers 1 through 8. Some of the numbers were BIG and some of the numbers were small. In line one, the numbers 1, 3, 5, and 7 were BIG and the numbers 2, 4, 6, and 8 were small.

Mrs. Boss said, "Class, I want you to play your instrument only on the BIG numbered beats in each line. On the small numbered beats, keep the instruments silent. Let's try playing the first line. Here we go! One, two, ready, play!" As she pointed to each numbered beat, the class played their instruments only on the BIG numbers. To keep everyone on the right beat, the students counted to 8 right along with Mrs. Boss.

"SUPER! Let's play all eight lines of the different beat patterns," said Mrs. Boss. Then she directed them through each beat of all eight lines as the children played their instruments. "EXCELLENT!" she said. "We are now ready to play the African beat rhythms with some music." The children's faces lit up with smiles!

Mrs. Boss turned on a computer program and music filled the room. Under their teacher's direction, the children played the different beat patterns line by line. It was a symphony of sound, with all the instruments playing together. Mrs. Boss played different pieces of music, from a folk song to a jazz piece. The children LOVED playing the different African beat patterns to the different styles of music. Grey Goose had fun too, as he learned to play the different instruments by being passed from child to child. What a FUN time in music class!

The following week, Mrs. Boss hid Grey Goose in the media center, at the book checkout desk. The children did not find Grey Goose until later in the week, when they went to media class. Lori was the one to find him, and she stuck her hand out to grab him. Taylor, Nicole, and Amanda ran over to Lori and hugged her.

Taylor said, "Lori found Grey Goose!" and Nicole and Amanda, both wearing their September birthday hats, clapped and grinned with delight!

"I'm taking Grey Goose to Mrs. Boss," said Lori. "She will be so HAPPY!"

When the children went to music, Lori gave Grey Goose to Mrs. Boss. The children clapped their hands so cheerfully.

Mrs. Boss asked, "What clue did you find this week as to what makes Harmony Park the BEST SCHOOL for one hundred million miles?"

The children all shouted, "BEST BOOKS!"

On the board where she'd written her question, Mrs. Boss added Best Books under Best Lunches. Then she turned around and said, "Harmony Park does have the BEST BOOKS, but there's another reason Harmony Park is the BEST SCHOOL for one hundred million miles. Keep searching!"

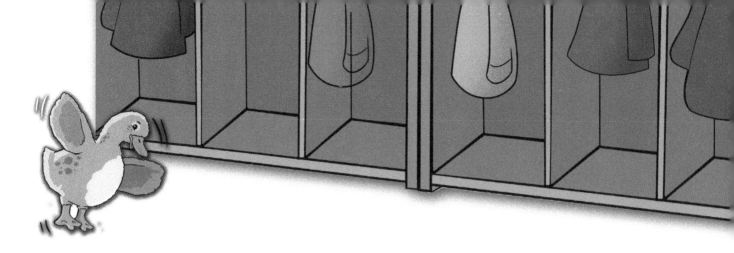

The following week Mrs. Mars, a teacher assistant, came in early to school and went right up to Mrs. Boss' music room. She had heard of the musical adventures of Grey Goose from some of the other teachers. So, Mrs. Mars asked Mrs. Boss if she could take Grey Goose and hide him in one of the children's cubbies in Mrs. Gerringer's room, just for fun. Mrs. Boss agreed that it was a great idea.

Mrs. Boss came to school the next day and did not see Grey Goose in the colorful, musical-note basket on her desk. She was missing Grey Goose already, but thought to herself that Grey Goose would be back soon.

A week passed and the children still had not found Grey Goose. This was because Grey Goose was in Wendell's cubby. Wendell had been absent all week due to getting ill with the chicken pox. When Mrs. Gerringer's class came to music class at the beginning of the week, they still had not found Grey Goose. Grey Goose was not in his home in the colorful, musical-note basket on Mrs. Boss' desk. Mrs. Boss did not know whose cubby Grey Goose was hiding in, so she told the class that Grey Goose must be on vacation.

When the class came to music at the end of the week, Mrs. Gerringer asked Mrs. Boss, "Have you seen your Grey Goose lately?"

Mrs. Boss replied, "No, Grey Goose has been gone for a long time! Have you seen Grey Goose?"

"No, but I know you really miss him. I hope he comes back really soon," replied Mrs. Gerringer.

Mrs. Boss said to the class, "Keep searching. Grey Goose is in the school somewhere. You'll find him." That day music class didn't feel the same without Grey Goose. The children missed Grey Goose. Grey Goose was missing from singing and dancing with the children.

The following week, Wendell finally returned to school. He reached his hand into his cubby and felt something soft and fuzzy. He squeezed the object and pulled it out quickly. The soft and fuzzy object was GREY GOOSE! Wendell danced around the room, holding up Grey Goose. He sang a song he had made up in his head.

Kinsley pointed at Wendell and shouted, "WHOA! LOOK EVERYBODY!"

Bob, John, Dave, Matt, and Bobby Junior each gave Wendell a high five to congratulate him. Wayne, Jim, Chris, Joe, Charlie, Martin, and Paul jumped up and down. They bumped into each other with excitement! Nancy and June twirled around in their new dresses, humming a happy, little tune. Colleen, Debbie, and Beverly cheered and clapped their hands! Kinsley, Kristy, Margaret, Nadine, Audrey, Trina, Anne, Jenny, and Susie each gave out a musical squeal of joy to show their glee! Gail, Jane, Kim, Janice, Sandy, Terri, Laurie, Joyce, Kris, and Vicky all hugged each other in a big group hug.

Lori, Taylor, Nicole, and Amanda jumped up and down. They pointed at Wendell and shouted, "WENDELL HAS GREY GOOSE!"

Bob said, "WAY TO GO, WENDELL!" as all the boys huddled around Wendell, patting his back.

"We're so PROUD of you!" said Nadine.

Kinsley, Kristy, Matt, John, and Bobby Junior started a chant saying, "WEN-DELL, WEN-DELL, WEN-DELL, WEN-DELL!" The chant got louder and louder. The rest of the class joined in, chanting and cheering. They gave each other fist bumps with excitement and JOY!

Mrs. Gerringer looked around the room at all the children in her class to see what all the excitement was about. The children rushed over to her and showed her Grey Goose.

John said, "WENDELL FOUND GREY GOOSE!"

Mrs. Gerringer said, "Mrs. Boss will be so HAPPY that you found her Grey Goose! She has been missing Grey Goose for a long time!"

Louise, Joan, and Diane, who loved to read books, replied, "What a HAPPY ending to our Grey Goose story!"

The children couldn't wait to return Grey Goose to Mrs. Boss. It was music day, so the children eagerly lined up. Then they followed Mrs. Gerringer in a single file line to the music room. Trina, who spoke two languages, Mandarin and English, started softly singing the "Harmony Park School Song" in Chinese. Upon hearing the melody, Kinsley, Kristy, Margaret, Nadine, Audrey, Joe, Anne, Jenny, and Susie joined in singing the song in English. One by one, everyone joined in, singing very softly. When Mrs. Gerringer's class finally arrived at the music room door, the children burst into singing louder. As they marched to their seats, Mrs. Boss rushed over to the piano to play the "Harmony Park School Song."

After the song was over, Mrs. Boss said, "You make my heart SING with JOY!" She congratulated the class on knowing the words and the melody to the song. "Your voices sound so beautiful when you sing together in unison!"

After clapping for her class, Mrs. Gerringer told Mrs. Boss that the children had a BIG SURPRISE for her. Wendell stood up and gave Grey Goose to Mrs. Boss. Mrs. Boss got a HUGE SMILE on her face. The children were so HAPPY to return Grey Goose to the music room.

Mrs. Boss said, "If you know this song . . ."

"Just sing along!" the children shouted.

Mrs. Boss sat down at the piano and started singing the "Harmony Park School Song" again. The children took turns singing and dancing with Grey Goose.

After the song, Mrs. Boss asked, "So, what clue did Grey Goose give you as to what makes Harmony Park the BEST SCHOOL for one hundred million miles?"

Kinsley asked, "Is our classroom the most important reason why Harmony Park is the BEST SCHOOL?"

The children yelled, "BEST CLASSROOMS!"

Mrs. Boss replied, "Well, let's see."

On the list under Best Books, which was under Best Lunches, Mrs. Boss wrote Best Classrooms.

Best Lunches
Best Books
Best Classrooms

37

All of a sudden, Mrs. Boss brought out a present and held it up for the class to see. "Inside this present is the answer to my question of what makes Harmony Park the BEST SCHOOL for one hundred million miles."

"OPEN IT, PLEASE! OPEN IT!" the children exclaimed with delight!

Mrs. Boss opened the present and inside was the answer.

In unison, all together, the children shouted, "A MIRROR?"

"YES!" Mrs. Boss replied.

The children looked confused. They didn't understand how a mirror could make Harmony Park the BEST SCHOOL for one hundred million miles.

Mrs. Boss continued. "YES, Harmony Park is the BEST SCHOOL for one hundred million miles because it has the BEST LUNCHES, the BEST BOOKS, and the BEST CLASSROOMS, but the most important reason is . . ."

rs. Boss took the mirror and panned it around the room so that every child saw his or her face in the mirror . . . even Grey Goose.

Mrs. Boss explained, "YOU are the reason Harmony Park is the BEST SCHOOL for one hundred million miles! All of you worked together as a team to find Grey Goose. Good for you! I am so PROUD of YOU! Without you, Grey Goose would not have been found. It is not the lunches or the books or the classrooms that make the school the best, even though they are all great! It is YOU who makes the school the BEST! In Harmony Park and in schools around the world, EVERY STUDENT makes EVERY SCHOOL the BEST, no matter where you go to school! You are all a part of the MUSIC inside my heart. So, let's celebrate YOU by singing, moving, playing instruments, creating, and reading music today with spirit!"

"Don't forget Grey Goose!" the children shouted.

Mrs. Boss said, "We certainly will not forget Grey Goose. Everyone can join in! So, if you know this song . . ."

"Just sing along!" the children shouted.

The children ended music class with the singing of the "Harmony Park School Song." They marched around the room to the steady beat. This time they sang with even more feeling than before. Their friend Grey Goose had returned!

40

Kinsley came home from school jumping for joy, as her friend the musical Grey Goose had been found! She told her mommy that Mrs. Boss was happy again as were all the children at Harmony Park Elementary School. Through the musical adventures of Grey Goose, Kinsley knew in her heart that her school was the BEST SCHOOL for one hundred million miles. It was the best because of her great teachers and all her nice friends. Kinsley beamed with delight because she knew that she was a part of the music inside Mrs. Boss' heart.

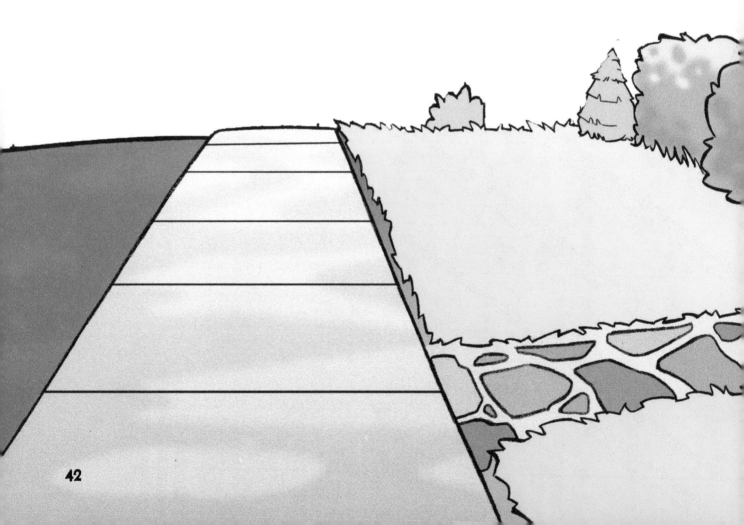

ACKNOWLEDGEMENTS

Words cannot express all the gratitude I feel in my heart to those who inspired, supported, and guided me in the process of publishing my book. I am forever grateful . . . THANK YOU!

To God, give all the glory! GOD IS SO GREAT! The Lord has blessed me with many gifts in my life. YOU are one of them. God planted the seed of creativity in my mind, and as a result, I wrote this book. THANK YOU, LORD! I've always LOVED writing, and having my children's book published is a dream come true for me with many prayers answered.

To my God-loving, nurturing parents, Bobby and Nadine Busbice; my loving, supportive husband, John; our children, Kristy and Matthew; our granddaughter, Kinsley; my brother, Wendell; my sister, Lori; our three nieces, Taylor, Nicole, and Amanda; and to all my family and friends for all your encouragement, praise, guidance, and support. You are the love of my life and in my heart forever.

To my dear friends Diane Pickeral, Anne Ward, Robin Strempek, Dave Bechtold, Nancy Wisner, DonnaMarie Fekete, Sally Albrecht, Jane Knighton, June Moody, and Louise Smith; my sister, Lori Fullmer; and my forever first reader, editor-in-chief, and husband, John Boss, for all your guidance, help, support, expertise, and time to guide me along on this book journey in your own special way. You are all angels in my life and words cannot begin to express the appreciation I feel in my heart for everything you've done for me. Many THANKS!

To the many dedicated music teachers that have touched my life—thank you. THANK YOU to my parents, Bobby and Nadine Busbice; my aunt Audrey and uncle Jimmie Foster; my grandmothers Virginia Clendening "Yonnie" and Ivie Busbice "Mother Busbice"; and my cousin Wayne Busbice, who all gave me my musical beginnings. I am grateful to my dedicated, brilliant music teachers: Rev. Sidney and Mrs. Jeannette Conger, Mrs. Martha Gaddy, Mr. James Basta, Mr. Harry Haywood, Mrs. Nancy Terrill, Mr. Dale Nonnemacher, Mr. Joe Richter, Dr. Leon Fleming, Dr. Sharon Lentz, Mr. John Palmer, Mr. Paul Lavin, and Dr. Roger "Doc" Folstrom; my fabulous, supportive music supervisors and facilitators: Joe Richter, Eugene Miller, Barbara King, Rob White, and Terry Eberhardt; and the excellent, outstanding Howard County Public School System in Maryland, of which I was a vocal music teacher for 32 years.

To all my friends at FriesenPress for your patience, guidance, knowledge, support, and help throughout the whole process of book publishing. THANK YOU, especially to my brilliant publishing specialist, Astra Crompton, and my terrific publishing team of Judith Hewlett, Nessa Pullman, Zuber Ahluwalia, Kara Anderson, and Ilsa Gurtins for everything! You've kept me on track, and your vision, expertise, knowledge, and excitement about the love of writing and book publishing is infectious! THANK YOU, ASTRA and PUBLISHING TEAM, YOU ARE THE BEST!

To my sensational FriesenPress editor, Rhonda Hayter, who has been my champion since day one. I appreciate your keen editorial eyes and unflagging support. My writing has improved because of your superb, indelible mark all over this book. Your words of praise, encouragement, guidance and ideas have enlightened my mind, brightened my spirit, and enriched my soul. I have learned so much from you!

To my outstanding, talented FriesenPress illustrator, Chad Thompson, who creatively designed each illustration to make the words of my manuscript come alive! YOU are INCREDIBLE, TALENTED, and AMAZING!

To my fabulous FriesenPress book designer, Teresita Hernandez, for designing the cover, back cover, and inside of the book, making the story flow from page to page. You've created a true children's book.

To Tammara Kennelly (President of FriesenPress), Dawn Johnston, Nicole LeBlanc, Debbie Anderson, and the many others at FriesenPress who have helped me behind the scenes. You've made my dream come true!

To the staff, students, and communities of Hammond, Guilford, and Bushy Park Elementary Schools in Howard County, Maryland, for your love and support throughout my career as a music teacher. You are family to me. In honor of you, I have named the fictitious school in the book, Harmony Park Elementary, after all three schools I have taught: "Harmony" for Hammond Elementary, "Park" for Bushy Park Elementary, and "Elementary" for Guilford Elementary.

To the late Beth Gerringer and Joan McCaw, both former kindergarten teachers and colleagues, and to the late Bobby Boss, Jr., my nephew, for being my inspiration in writing this book. We love and miss you dearly.

To all my many talented, musical students I've taught, you have been an inspiration to me, more than you know. I hope you recognize bits and pieces from the book and journey back into the world of elementary school, back into music, as the memories of our musical experiences together have truly blessed my heart. THANKS for the "BLAST FROM THE PAST!"

To all of you who read my book, THANK YOU! You make my heart SING with JOY!

You are all a part of the MUSIC inside my heart.

CPSIA information can be obtained
at www.ICGtesting.com
Printed in the USA
LVHW071424091220
672134LV00031BA/963